THE PRINCESS STORYBOOK

The Princess Storybook

FIVE FAVORITE FAIRY TALES ADAPTED BY JULIA SUMMERS

WITH PAINTINGS AND DRAWINGS BY
STEVE CARTER, FERNANDO CASINI, BECKY FINDLAY,
MERRILY JOHNSON AND ARLENE NOEL
DESIGNED BY BRUCE BAKER

HALLMARK CHILDREN'S EDITIONS

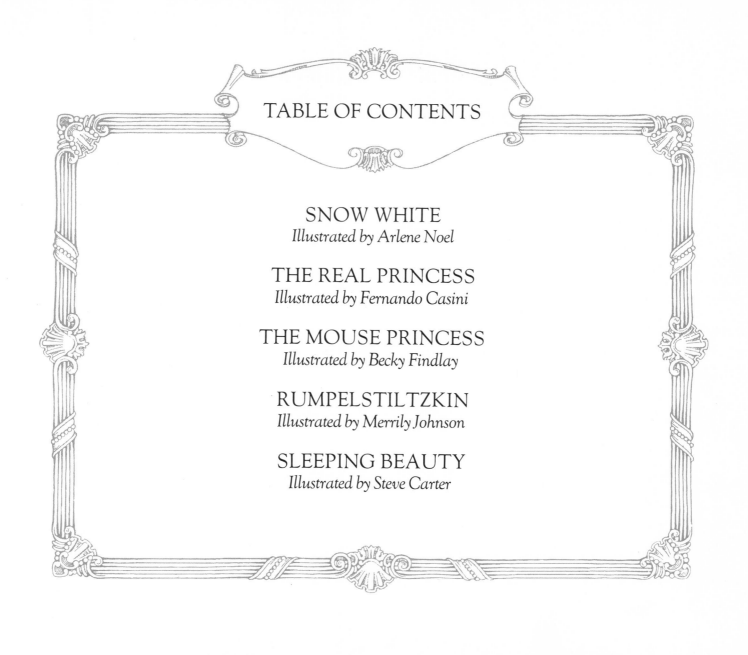

TABLE OF CONTENTS

SNOW WHITE

LONG AGO IN A FARAWAY LAND, a royal child was born who was named Snow White. Soon afterwards, her mother, the queen, grew ill and died.

In time the king married again. The new queen was very beautiful, but selfish and vain. Her greatest delight was a magic

mirror. Every morning and evening the queen would ask:

> *"Mirror, mirror on the wall,*
> *Who is the fairest one of all?"*

And the mirror would answer:

> *"You are the fairest one of all!"*

Years passed, and Snow White grew to be as pretty as a picture. The queen could not help noticing, and one day when she asked her mirror who was the fairest in the land, it replied:

> *"Though you have*
> *a beauty that is rare,*
> *Snow White is a thousand*
> *times more fair."*

The queen flew into a rage! She could not stand to have anyone around who was more beautiful than she. So she ordered one of the king's hunters to take Snow White far into the woods and kill her. The hunter took Snow White into the woods, but he was a kind man and he did not hurt her. He gave her some food and even pointed out a path that led into another kingdom.

Snow White grew afraid in the deep, dark woods full of strange noises and wild animals. In no time she became hopelessly lost.

Just at sunset, when she was too tired to go a step farther, Snow White came upon a little cottage. Inside she found seven of everything—seven little chairs, and even seven little beds! She tried out each bed, and the last one seemed just right. She pulled the covers up around her chin and fell fast asleep.

A short time later, the owners of the little cottage came home. They were seven dwarfs who worked on the hillsides digging for gold and gems.

"My goodness," said the first dwarf, "someone has been in my bed!"

"Mine too!" cried the second dwarf. "My blanket is upside down!"

"Mine too," said the third dwarf. "And mine," exclaimed the fourth, fifth and sixth dwarfs.

And the seventh dwarf jumped back and cried, "Someone *is* in my bed!"

The dwarfs thought about waking Snow White. But she looked so beautiful and was sleeping so peacefully that they decided not to disturb her.

In the morning, when Snow White awoke and saw the seven dwarfs, she almost ran away. But the woods scared her more than the dwarfs. When they got up, they smiled at her and she told them her story. It made the dwarfs so sad that they said she could stay with them in return for cooking and keeping the cottage neat and clean.

days and weeks passed, and White lived happily in the cottage in the deep, dark woods.

Meanwhile, the queen, who thought Snow White was dead, one day asked her mirror:

"Mirror, mirror on the wall,
Who is the fairest one of all?"

And to her surprise, the mirror said:

"Though you have
a beauty that is rare,
Snow White is a thousand
times more fair."

The wicked queen called in the king's hunter, who confessed he had let Snow White go. Angrily the queen asked the mirror where Snow White was, and it told her about the dwarfs.

Then the queen dressed herself up in a ragged coat, made up her face to look like an old woman and put on a stringy wig. She fixed a basket with fruit and right on top put an apple with poison on one side of it. "Apples, oranges, bananas for sale!" she cried when she reached the dwarfs' cottage. The dwarfs had warned Snow White to beware of strangers while they were away at work. But the woman looked harmless enough. And the apple looked so delicious! When the woman took a bite out of it, Snow White thought certainly it must be all right. But as soon as she took a bite herself, she fell down as if dead.

The dwarfs returned that evening and found Snow White lying on the floor. They tried everything to wake her up, but nothing worked.

In the castle, when the queen asked the mirror who was the fairest one of all, it answered:

"You, Queen, are the
fairest one of all!"

The dwarfs watched Snow White for three days. She remained as beautiful as ever, but she did not wake up. So, very sadly, they built a coffin out of glass. They placed Snow White in it and then put the coffin under a shady tree where they could always see her.

For many years Snow White lay in the glass coffin. The dwarfs kept guard over her and from time to time looked closely at her in case she might come back to life again. But Snow White never moved.

Then one day a handsome prince came through the woods. When he saw Snow White he was overcome by her beauty and immediately fell in love with her. He pleaded with the dwarfs to let him take Snow White. "I cannot live without her," he said, "for she is the most beautiful girl in all the land."

At last the dwarfs felt so sorry for the prince that they allowed him to take Snow White. He called his servants to carry the glass coffin, but in picking it up, one of them stumbled and fell. The accident knocked the piece of poison apple from Snow White's mouth.

Her eyes fluttered open. Slowly she sat up. "She's alive!" cried the dwarfs, and they danced for joy around the cottage. And when Snow White saw the prince, she fell in love with him just as he had with her, and they went off together to be married.

When the wicked queen heard about the wedding and the beautiful bride, she ran to the mirror, asking:

"Am I not the fairest one of all?"
And the mirror replied:

*"Queen, that is no longer true.
Snow White is more beautiful than you!"*
Then the queen broke the mirror and flew into such a rage that she fell over backwards down the huge stairway and was killed.

Snow White and the prince were married, and they lived happily in a great castle. But as often as possible, they went out into the woods to visit their very best friends — the seven dwarfs.

The Real Princess

Once there was a prince who wanted to marry a princess. He traveled all over the world trying to find a princess who was a *real* princess. He met plenty of princesses, but he had a hard time deciding which of them was a *real* princess. There was always something that didn't seem quite right. So finally the prince returned to his home, very tired and very discouraged.

That same night a terrible storm blew up. Rain poured, wind roared, lightning flashed, and the prince and his family barely heard a knock at the castle door. The king himself opened it, and there stood the most bedraggled girl you could ever imagine. Her hair dripped in stringy bunches around her face. Her clothes were stuck against her legs with mud. Her shoes were full of water and sloshed when she walked. But she said she was a real princess.

The queen invited her to spend the night in the castle. She thought to herself, "We'll just see if she's a real princess or not."

The queen went to the bedroom where the girl was to sleep and put a pea on the very bottom of the bed. Then she piled twenty mattresses on top of the pea. She piled twenty featherbeds on top of the mattresses. The next morning the queen asked the princess how she had slept.

"I hardly slept at all," the girl replied grumpily. "There was some hard thing in my bed, and I'm bruised black and blue from sleeping on it. It was just terrible!"

The queen and king and prince looked at each other and all three said at once, "She's a *real princess!*" For only a *real* princess could have skin delicate enough to feel the pea through all those mattresses and featherbeds.

So the prince and the real princess were married and lived happily for many years. And the pea was placed in the royal museum, where it may be seen to this day.

THE MOUSE PRINCESS

LONG AGO IN THE DAYS OF WITCHES AND MAGIC, there lived a beautiful princess. One day while she was playing in the forest, she accidentally stepped on the long nose of a witch who was napping under a log. The witch was so angry that she changed the princess into a mouse! "And a mouse you shall stay," she screamed, "until the day you make me laugh!" ❊ The mouse princess was so frightened that she ran far, far away. Finally, in the land of Skitterlee, she found an old deserted castle. There she lived for several years. ❊ The king of Skitterlee had three sons. Two were witty and fun loving, while the youngest was shy and quiet. The king could not decide which one should take over the throne. He did know, however, that whoever it was must have a perfect wife — a queen who would be patient, wise, skilled…and beautiful. He sent for his sons and gave each of them a piece of flax. "Take this flax to the lady of your choice. Have her spin it into thread and make a piece of cloth so fine that I can draw one hundred yards of it through my golden ring." The two older sons were in love with beautiful daughters of noblemen. Neither of these rich ladies had ever learned to make cloth, but they wanted to be queen more than anything else and so they went to work at once. The young son did not have a maiden to love. He was too shy and preferred the company of gentle animals. Sadly he walked into the woods thinking there was no one to spin his flax into cloth. Presently he came to the castle where the mouse princess lived. When she saw him sit down looking so unhappy, she scurried up to him

and asked, "What is making you so sad?" The prince gladly told her. "Well," she said, "that's not so bad. Leave the flax with me and return in seven days." So he thanked her kindly, and after visiting for an hour or so, he left, thinking what an interesting companion the little mouse was.

When the prince returned in seven days, the mouse princess was waiting. The prince was very glad to see her again. They talked of this and that, enjoying each other's company ever so much. Finally, as the last rays of sun began to sink from sight, the prince stood up to leave. The mouse princess handed him a small box. "Good luck," she said. "You will make a fine king." That night the older sons handed their father the cloth their sweethearts had woven. One piece was so stiff and coarse it could almost stand up by itself. It would not pass through the king's ring at all. The other piece was as loose as a fisherman's net and the ring became tangled up in it. ❀ Then the youngest son handed the king the small box. Out of it the king pulled yard after yard of cloth so soft and fine that it easily passed through the ring. "The lady of your choice is indeed patient, wise and skilled," said the king. "However, I cannot decide who shall be queen until I have seen each lady in person. At sundown tonight, bring them here. Then I shall tell you whom I have chosen as queen and thus, who shall be the next king." ❀ The young prince returned to the forest feeling very sad. How could he bring his little friend to meet a king? But he yearned to see her anyhow himself and walked on to the old castle. ❀ The mouse princess ran to greet him and scampered onto a sundial beside the prince. "How did your father like the cloth?" she asked. ❀ "He liked it very much. But now he would meet the lady who spun it. I only came back to thank you and to give you this ring. You're the best friend I ever had." ❀ The mouse princess sat very quietly for a moment. When she lifted her eyes, the prince could see that they were filled with tears. "Do you trust me?" she asked. ❀ "You know I do," he assured her. ❀ "Then

return home very slowly. No matter what happens, do not turn around until you reach the gates of your castle." As soon as he was out of sight, the mouse scampered to a nearby farmyard and borrowed a fine black rooster. Quickly she made a bridle out of braided grass and a saddle out of an oak leaf. She mounted the rooster and hurried after the prince.

Now it happened that the witch who had cast the spell upon the princess lived on the road to the castle. When the witch looked out her window and saw a mouse riding on a rooster, she burst into laughter. Of course, as soon as the witch laughed, the mouse became a princess again, dressed in silk and pearls and riding on a beautiful black horse. The prince heard the laughter, but remembering his promise to the mouse, he did not turn around. When he entered the gates of the castle, he wondered why everyone was staring behind him and cheering. Then he remembered that he could now turn around, and there behind him was the most beautiful lady he had ever seen. Smiling, she rode past him, right up to the king, who helped her off her horse. ❧ She was so beautiful, it was no surprise to anyone when the king put the queen's crown upon her head. ❧ As the puzzled prince walked up to her, she held out the ring he had given her. At once he recognized his mouse friend and understood. He put the ring on her finger and kissed her, and thereafter they ruled wisely and well as king and queen of Skitterlee for a long, long time.

Rumpelstiltzkin

*T*HERE WAS ONCE UPON A TIME a king who was so poor that he had no crown to wear and no throne to sit upon. He had no money in his treasury and no soldiers in his army. But he had one thing of great value, and that was his beautiful daughter, Gwendolyn.

Gwendolyn was as beautiful as her father was poor, and the king bragged about her to anyone who would listen. He was so proud of her that he even claimed she could spin straw into gold.

When a neighboring king heard of this boast, he sent for Gwendolyn and her father. Upon their arrival, he took the beautiful princess to a room filled with straw and said, "If you can truly spin this straw into gold, I shall restore your father's wealth. But if you do not, I shall have your father's life."

With that, he closed the door and locked it, leaving Gwendolyn to her misery. "What in the world will I do?" she cried, "I love my father dearly, but I haven't the least idea how to spin straw into gold."

As she sat weeping, a strange little man came hopping through the window. "Good evening, my dear princess," he cackled. "Why are you crying?"

Gwendolyn told her story. "And I haven't the least idea," she said again, "how to spin straw into gold."

"Don't cry, for it is a simple matter when you know how. If I spin the straw into gold for you, what will you give me?" asked the little man.

Gwendolyn wiped her eyes. "I don't have very much," she said, "but if you can truly do as you say, I will give you my mother's ruby necklace."

"Very well," he agreed and set to work.

Whir, whir, whir went the wheel. Sure enough, the bobbin was full of gold! Whir, whir, whir went the wheel all through the night. When morning came, the straw was gone and the room was full of gold!

When the king came into the room, he was delighted. "Your father was telling the truth after all!" he cried. "I shall keep my promise and restore his riches. And now, my beautiful princess, come with me."

The king took Gwendolyn into another room full of straw which was even bigger than the first. "If you will spin all this into gold by morning, I shall restore your father's army. But if you fail, I shall have his life."

Again Gwendolyn began to cry. Surely there was no way to save her father this time.

But as before, the little man appeared at the window. "What will you give me now if I spin the straw into gold?"

Gwendolyn thought and thought. Then she remembered the sapphire ring her father had given her on her sixteenth birthday.

The little man took the ring. Whir, whir, whir went the spinning wheel. By morning, the room was full of glittering gold.

Merrily Johnson

The king was pleased beyond measure and, according to his promise, restored her father's armies. But still he was not satisfied. He took Gwendolyn into an even larger room and said, "If you spin all this into gold before morning, I will make you my wife." And he left the room and locked the door.

No sooner was he gone than the little man appeared at the window. "What will you give me this time if I spin the straw into gold?"

"I have nothing left to give," answered the girl honestly.

"Then promise me that you will give me your first child when you become queen."

The princess hesitated. That was a terrible thing to ask, she thought. But perhaps she would never have a child. And there seemed to be no other way out.

She agreed to his request. Whir, whir, whir went the spinning wheel, and once more the room was filled with gold by morning.

True to his word, the king married the princess. When a year had passed, she gave birth to a beautiful son.

Gwendolyn had almost forgotten the little man until one day he stepped into the garden where she was playing with her child. "I've come for your son," he announced. "Give him to me."

Gwendolyn was heartbroken. She offered him all the riches in the kingdom if he would let her keep the child.

"I don't want riches," he insisted. "I only want the child."

The queen began to cry so bitterly that he felt sorry for her and said, "I'll give you three days to guess my name, and if you succeed, you may keep the child."

Gwendolyn started at once to make a list of all the names she could think of. She sent messengers to travel all over the kingdom looking for unusual names.

When the little man arrived the next day, she started reading her list. "Is it Malcolm?" "No!" "Is it Zippo?" "No!" "Is it Jeremy?" "No!" At last she had read every name on her list, and the little man laughed and laughed as he left the palace.

On the second day, she read her list of unusual and uncommon names. "Is it Coriantumr or Zarahemla or Mergatroid?" At each name the little man shook his head, and when the sun went down, he went away laughing.

On the third day, one of the messengers returned and told the queen, "I have been to the end of the earth where the foxes and rabbits are friends. There I saw a little house, and in front of the house burned a little fire, and in front of the fire danced a little man who was singing:

> *"Tomorrow I'll stew, tomorrow I'll bake,*
> *For then the queen's child I shall take,*
> *For little dreams that royal dame*
> *That Rumpelstiltzkin is my name!"*

Imagine how happy the queen was! When the little man arrived, she asked, "Is your name Percival?"

"No!" "Is your name Hephzibah?"

"No!" "Is it by any chance Rumpelstiltzkin?"

The little man jumped up and down in a rage. "Some witch has told you! Some witch has told you!" he screamed. And then he stamped his foot so far into the ground that he disappeared from sight and was never heard from again!

Sleeping Beauty

LONG AGO AND FAR AWAY
there lived a king and queen
who were very unhappy.
They wanted a child more than anything
but didn't have one.
Then one bright, beautiful day
a baby girl was born.

The king and queen were so joyful they decided to have a big party to celebrate. All their friends and relatives were invited, and all the fairies in the kingdom were to be the guests of honor.

At one time there had been eight fairies in the kingdom. Years ago, however, the oldest fairy had disappeared, and so only the other seven were invited. The king had a golden knife, fork and spoon, each inlaid with precious jewels, made as a gift for each of the fairies and set at her place at the table.

After the feast was over, the fairies began to give their own gifts to the baby princess. One gave her beauty, another grace, the third a charming personality, the fourth good health, the fifth wit, and the sixth talent. Just as the seventh fairy was about to present her gift, into the hall stormed the oldest fairy anyone had ever seen!

She was the eighth fairy — the one everyone had forgotten about. Her feelings were hurt because she had been forgotten, and even more hurt when she saw the lovely gifts the king had given the other fairies. So she stamped her foot and shouted, "When the young princess is sixteen years old, she will prick her finger on the spindle of a spinning wheel and fall down dead!" Then she stomped out of the castle as suddenly as she had come.

Everyone was shocked, and the queen began to cry. Then the seventh fairy stood up and said, "While I cannot undo this curse, I can make it easier. The princess will prick her finger on a spindle, but she will not die. Instead, she will fall into a deep sleep lasting a hundred years and will be awakened by a prince."

The king, naturally, wanted to protect his daughter from the curse; so he ordered every spindle in the kingdom burned and made it illegal to own one.

The princess grew to be a charming girl, and everyone loved her very much. It happened that on her sixteenth birthday, the king and queen had to spend the day outside the castle on royal business. The princess decided to entertain herself by exploring the castle. She wandered up and up into one of the towers until she came to a room she had never seen before. Inside she found an old woman spinning with a spinning wheel and spindle. The woman had not heard the king's command that all spindles must be destroyed. The princess, who had never before seen anyone spinning, asked the woman what she was doing.

"I'm spinning, my dear," she replied. "Would you like to try it?"

The princess reached out to take the spindle. The moment it touched her finger, it pricked her skin, and she slumped down onto a nearby bed and fell into a deep sleep.

Sleep immediately spread over the whole castle. The maids and cooks fell asleep. The guards and dogs fell asleep. Butterflies fluttered to the ground asleep. Even the fire on which dinner was cooking fell asleep. Just then the king and queen returned to the castle, and they immediately fell asleep, too. Within just a few minutes, a tall wall of thorny bushes grew up around the castle, so thick that no one could get through it.

The sleeping castle stayed this way for a hundred years. Then one day a handsome young prince came riding by. He stopped when he saw the huge wall of bushes and asked a group of men what it was. One told him that it was a castle enchanted by witches. Another said that no one lived there. Then an old man stepped up and said, "Sir, I heard my father say that his father told him a beautiful young princess who is called Sleeping Beauty and all her family lie asleep inside, and that a young prince will awaken her when she has slept a hundred years." This story intrigued the prince, and he decided he would try to get inside. As he went riding up to the castle, the bushes magically parted in front of him and let him through. He was surprised and a little frightened to see that they closed again behind him.

When he reached the courtyard, he found everyone asleep. It was so quiet he could hear his own breathing. He searched all over the castle for Sleeping Beauty. When he finally found her, he was amazed at her loveliness. He stood looking at her for a few minutes, then leaned over and gently kissed her. Sleeping Beauty slowly opened her eyes and smiled up at the prince. Immediately they fell in love.

As soon as the princess awoke, everyone else began to awaken, too. The maids and cooks awoke. The guards and dogs awoke. Butterflies stretched their wings and began to fly in the sunshine. Even the fire on which dinner was cooking sputtered awake.

Since everyone was very, very hungry, a big feast was prepared. After the dinner, they went to the castle chapel, where the prince and princess were married. In time they became king and queen, ruled the little country well and lived happily the rest of their lives.